Bridget Greenwood
Illustrations by Abbie Hart

SuperMax - The Thirdhand Hound

Bumblebee Books
London

A CIP catalogue record for this title is
available from the British Library.

ISBN: 978-1-83934-470-1

Bumblebee Books is an imprint of
Olympia Publishers.

First Published in 2021

Bumblebee Books
Tallis House
2 Tallis Street
London
EC4Y 0AB

Printed in Great Britain

www.olympiapublishers.com

Dedication

For Emily and Jack x

"How long? How long until we get there?"

Max was going to the beach. Any walk was good but the beach was the best.

No sooner had the car stopped and the latch of the boot sprung open Max was out, joining in the kerfuffle. There were dads and babies, teenagers kicking balls, dogs with sticks, fisherman with long rods reaching out in to the sea, gaggles of seagulls marching menacingly forward. Max liked to chase the seagulls, defending all the ice creams and chips about to be taken. Super Hero Max!

Sometimes Max forgot to look and listen and today was no exception.
All of a sudden Max realised he was all alone.
No more seagulls or muddles of people.
Suddenly Max didn't feel quite so brave.

Max made his way along the beach. All of a sudden something very small caught his eye, bustling about, busily flipping stones over and over.

"Hello," said Max, "who are you?"

"I am a turnstone," said the little bird. "I flip the stones looking for food."

Max tried flipping a stone but there were no sausages or sandwiches underneath.

"I'm all alone, just like you," said Max. "Shall we journey on together?"

With that a whole flock of camouflaged turnstones spun round and opened their wings, revealing a uniform of white stripes.

"Oh no," said the bird, "I am not alone, we are a team, my friends and I. Teamwork makes the dream work don't you know."

With that the birds swooped up into the air like a formation of RAF airplanes.

Max continued his journey… alone.

A little further along the way Max could see something wriggling and squiggling backwards and forwards in the sand.

"Hello," said Max, "are you all alone?"

"No, no," said the rock salmon. "I'm just trying to get back to my friends in the sea. The sea has been very rough you see and somehow I ended up out of the sea."

"Oh dear," said Max, "shall we journey on together then?"

"Oh no," said the rock salmon, "never give up. I will try and try, wriggling and squiggling until I am back where I belong."

And with that a huge wave came and took the rock salmon back to his friends. The wave covered Max's feet too but when it had gone Max was still standing on the sand... alone

Max decided he wouldn't give up either and he journeyed on... alone.

Just around the next corner Max froze in his steps for bowling towards him were four enormous basset hounds! Max took a big gulp and stood firm.

He needn't have worried. "Hello, little thing," said Molly, the leader of the pack as she towered over Max.

Next up was Mabel, "Cooee, darling, shall we play?"

Maggie and Maisy were next. "Wait for us, darlings. Oh hello, little man."

Max suddenly felt so much better, a big smile spread across his face.

Max began to bounce around between the girls, barking and darting back and forth.

"Oh what joy," said Maggie. "What fun." The melee continued until the girls ground to a halt and sat down.

"Enough, enough," said Maisy. "Girls, look." The four bassets could see their owner, Mia, strolling ahead. "Darling we have to go but such fun, come on, girls, Mia is waiting."

"Shall I come too?" asked Max.

"Oh no," the girls laughed. "You must go with your own owner."

But that was the thing, Max had lost his owner and he continued on… alone.

Max journeyed on along the sand. What was that he could see rising up in the shallows?

A row of jagged spikes curled its way out of the waves. Was it a dinosaur Max wondered?

Momentarily he froze wondering if he was in any danger. The waves washed to and fro, revealing more and more of its secrets.

Just along the way a row of what looked like soldiers were climbing out of the water.

Max sat for a while and watched the rhythm of the tide and then he could see it clearly! Max felt a little foolish, his imagination had been running away with him. There were, of course, no dinosaurs or soldiers on the beach. Only shipwrecks and groynes, sturdy barriers protecting the beach and giving shelter to all sorts of crabs and shells and pebbles, shiny and glistening. The treasure of the sea.

Suddenly Max realised he didn't feel quite so alone. There was a whole lot of life down there!

Suddenly, completely destroying his quiet contemplation, a small puppy bounced right up to Max and playfully crouched in front of him wanting to play.

"Hello," said the pup, "I'm Monty." Monty was wearing a brightly coloured jumper, all the colours of the rainbow. Max wished he had a jumper.

"Shall we play?" asked Monty and with that Max and Monty were racing up and down along the shore, darting in and out of the waves. The game went on for ages, from the distance Max could hear, "Monty… Monty… come here." Max could hear a certain anxiousness in the voice. He looked round and saw Monty's owners. Max thought for a moment and then walked towards the voice, bringing Monty with him. They both sat down in front of Monty's relieved owner who rewarded them both with a biscuit.

"Hello, Monty, and hello you, little fella. Thank you for bringing Monty back." Monty's owner patted the top of Max's head, scooped up Monty and wandered back up the beach.

Max sat and enjoyed his reward.

After finishing his biscuit, on he went, further along the beach. Max realised that he was getting tired now.

Sitting further up the beach was a dad with a toddler having a picnic. Max thought that looked like a jolly good idea and wandered up to say hello.

"Hello, boy," was the warm, friendly welcome he received and another gentle pat on his head. Things were definitely looking up! Max sat, smiling at the little boy who was holding out a triangle of ham sandwich.

Gratefully Max accepted the gift and sat contentedly and then the most amazing thing happened. Along the beach came Jack, Max's owner.

"There you are, Max. Have you had fun?"

Max began to bounce and spin and bark and bounced right in to Jack's arms.

On the way home Max thought about his adventures and realised what fun he had had, meeting lots of new friends and learning lots of new things. Feeling happy and sad and frightened and brave all at the same time but most of all Max realised how much he loved Jack and later that evening Max curled up on Jack's lap in front of the fire and went for a very, very long sleep.

About the Author

From the age of seven I announced that I would write and here I am at the beginning of my literary journey, having spent a lifetime enjoying books and reading I give to you *SuperMax*. I live with my dog in a rural cottage in the South East of England. I have two grown up children and work as a school business manager for a secondary college and have worked in education for twenty-five years.

Acknowledgements

Thank you to Abbie Hart whose wonderful illustrations bring Max to life and of course Max.

Printed in Great Britain
by Amazon